The Greedy Crows

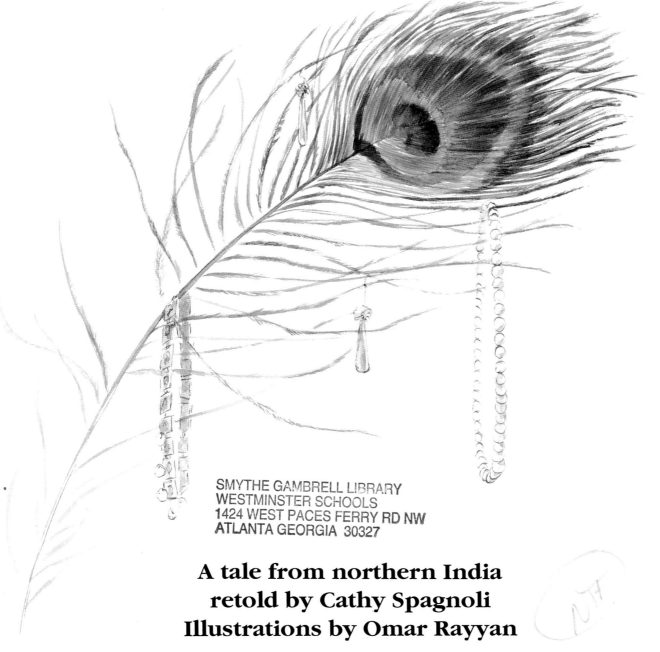

A tale from northern India
retold by Cathy Spagnoli
Illustrations by Omar Rayyan

Once, in India, a peacock lived a simple life near a crow and his six crow sisters. Every day, the peacock and the crow would go to the forest to fetch firewood. But the peacock wanted only a few pieces, while the crow craved huge piles of wood—as did his five greedy sisters, who always cawed, "More! More! More!"

2

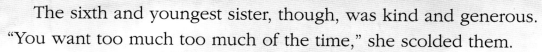

The sixth and youngest sister, though, was kind and generous.
"You want too much too much of the time," she scolded them.

Her words pleased the peacock, who often shared his wood
with her. She in turn served him soft chapatti bread
and sweet mangoes.

Then one day in the forest, the peacock stepped on a thorn.

"Ohhh, Brother Crow," he pleaded. "Please take this out."

But the crow ignored him.

"Do pull out the thorn," begged the peacock.

But the crow still ignored him.

"My friend, it hurts so," cried the peacock.

"I'm too busy.
 The light is poor.
  My eyes are weak.
   My claws are too big," replied the crow at last.
"But I'll take your wood, since you won't need it."
 And off he flew, well pleased and well loaded,
leaving the peacock all alone.

Just then, the peacock heard drums:

Ta din din na! Ta din din na!

A wedding party came riding by in a festive cart.
He leaped on it, next to the bride and groom.

"Your turban looks most elegant on your head,"
he said to the groom. "I too have a crown. We are alike.
So please pull out my thorn."

When the groom turned away, the peacock swayed
to face the bride.

"Your jewels look most splendid on your neck. I too have
feather jewels. We are alike. So please pull out my thorn."

"UGH! YOU'RE FILTHY!" she shrieked.

But as the cart bounced on, the peacock
   slo-o-o-owly,
     slo-o-o-owly spread his feathers.
And slo-o-owly a smile spread across the bride's face.
"He truly does look like a king now," she whispered.

"Let us hang my jewels on him."
So the two draped shining toe rings, anklets of bells,
golden lotus chains, and strings of pearls all over him.
"How sweet! How sweet!" they cried.

They beamed and clapped, but the peacock
flapped his gleaming wings and rose up into the sky.
"Come back, come back!" they cried.
"We'll help you now. Come back!"
But the peacock, richly robed, vanished from view.

On and on he flew until the homes of the crows
glowed ahead.

Just then, the night frowned and hurled down hail
as big as marbles.

The peacock stumbled to the house of the eldest sister.
"PLEASE OPEN YOUR DOOR," he cried.
"I'm Friend Peacock, and the hail hurts me so."
"Go away," croaked a cranky voice.

He fled to the next sister's house.

"PLEASE OPEN YOUR DOOR," he cried.

"I'm Friend Peacock, and the hail hurts me so."

"No, no," she shrilled. "I'm busy."

And on he went to the next sister's house.

"PLEASE OPEN YOUR DOOR," he cried.

"I'm Friend Peacock, and the hail hurts me so."

"Oh, quiet! My head aches," replied the crow.

On to the fourth and the fifth sister's houses he went.

But no one opened a door.

Finally, the peacock fell in front of the youngest
sister's home, moaning, "Help me, please."
Immediately the door jumped open.
"Come in, dear brother," invited the crow.

Carefully, she sat him down,
pulled out the thorn,
and served him sweet milk.

The peacock relaxed, gazed at her courtyard, and spoke.
"Dear friend, please sweep the floor." So she did.
"Dear friend, please draw patterns on it." So she did.
"Dear friend, please scatter roses about." So she did.
"Dear friend, please light the oil lamps." So she did.

"Now, sing a soft song."
And she sang in tones that lulled the night:
   "Sa, sa-ri, sa-ri,
      sa-ri-ga, sa-ri-ga,
         sa-ri-ga-ma."

The peacock, with regal grace, stepped into the courtyard.
Above, the moon glowed—a royal white umbrella.
Below, petals and patterns spread—a royal carpet.
"Friend Crow," he said, "tell me your wish:
My feathers—to the right or to the left?"
"As you like," she replied.

And so—
to the right, *ta ki ta, ki ta, ta ka;*
to the left, *ta ki ta, ki ta, ta ka*—
he spread his tail and danced.

To the right, *ta ki ta, ki ta, ta ka;*
to the left, *ta ki ta, ki ta, ta ka*—
he danced and danced and danced.
    And as his feathers quivered proudly, out spilled gold and gems.
    "For you, my friend," he said at the end.
    Then he sipped warm milk and returned to his home in peace.

Dawn crept up in a garland of light. The greedy crows
greeted the sun and soon heard of their sister's new wealth.
"Hurry! Hurry!" they squawked to their brother.
"Go find that bride and bring us jewels, too!"

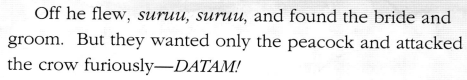

Off he flew, *suruu, suruu*, and found the bride and groom. But they wanted only the peacock and attacked the crow furiously—*DATAM!*

DATAM!

DATAM!

When the crow didn't return, the sisters hopped to the peacock.
"Dearest brother," they cried, "last night, we misunderstood you.
Do come to our homes today and be our honored guest."

On and on they pleaded
until at last he agreed.

That evening, when the peacock returned from the woods,
he went to the eldest sister's home.

"Come in, dear friend," she crooned. "Drink sweet milk;
then hurry and dance!"

He stepped into a courtyard bright with lamps and colors.

"My feathers—to the right or to the left?" he asked.

"Both! Both! Quickly!" she cried.

And so—to the right, *ta ki ta, ki ta, ta ka;*

to the left, *ta ki ta, ki ta, ta ka*—he spread his tail and danced.

To the right, *ta ki ta, ki ta, ta ka;*

to the left, *ta ki ta, ki ta, ta ka*—he danced.

But this time—no jewels.

Only spiders, scorpions, snakes, and centipedes,
who rushed to bite the greedy crow's feet!

As the crow tried to escape, the peacock walked
to the next house.

"Come in, dear friend," sang the second sister.
"Drink sweet milk, then hurry and dance!"
He stepped into a courtyard bright with lamps and colors.
"My feathers—to the right or to the left?" he asked.
"Both! Both! Quickly!" she cried.
And so—to the right, *ta ki ta, ki ta, ta ka;*
to the left, *ta ki ta, ki ta, ta ka*—he spread his tail and danced.
To the right—*ta ki ta, ki ta, ta ka;*
to the left, *ta ki ta, ki ta, ta ka*—he danced.
And more crawly creatures chased her, too.

And so it was with the third, the fourth, and the fifth sisters.

Finally, finished with his work, the peacock stayed with the last sister.

And they were never again bothered by the greedy crows, who had learned their lesson well.

Thus the peacock and the kind crow lived happily together for a very long time.